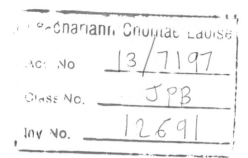

MYRIAD BOOKS LIMITED
35 Bishopsthorpe Road, London SE26 4PA

First published in 2002 by
MIJADE PUBLICATIONS
16-18, rue de l'Ouvrage, 5000 Namur-Belgium

ISBN 1 84746 105 0
EAN 978 1 84746 105 6

Printed in China

Stéphanie Blanchart

Norbert
and the disappearing eggs

MYRIAD BOOKS LIMITED

It was a beautiful sunny morning.
Norbert the wild duck came out of
the reeds where he had spent the night
and shook his wings. He was still numb
from sleeping. It was time to have breakfast!
Just as he walked to the edge of the pond
he heard a rustling of leaves…

Rick the Fox burst out of the bushes
and leaped towards him.
"I knew the day would come when
I would catch you!" Rick shouted.

"Come on, you don't really want to eat me, do you?"
Norbert protested. "I am so old and tasteless! Believe me!
Haven't you got anything more tender to chew on?"

Rick thought for a moment.
Over on the farm, Mrs Pinchbeak
had just laid four beautiful eggs.
Once they were born the baby
geese would be a treat, if somehow
he could just get hold of them.

"Listen to me, you old geezer!" said Rick.
"If you bring me Mrs Pinchbeak's baby birds you
won't have to worry about me any more! I'll leave
you alone until the day you die. What do you think of that?"
"It's a deal!" Norbert said, getting back on to his feet.

After Rick disappeared Norbert flew over to the farm.

Sometimes he joined the geese and hens at dinner time so he knew the layout of the farm well.

He crept into the deserted shed and found Mrs Pinchbeak's eggs.

"Much easier to carry than baby geese," said Norbert. He grabbed an old sack and popped the four eggs into it.

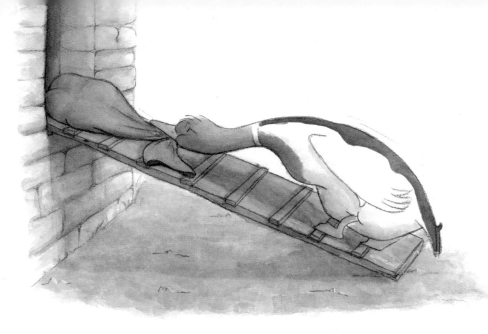

He dragged the sack down the ramp leading to the shed.

Then he grabbed the sack in his beak and ran quickly along the edge of the farmyard until he found a hole in the wall. Norbert crawled through and ran off into the woods.

Back at the pond Norbert built a nest and was just about to put the eggs in it when he heard a loud voice behind him. It was his friend Ginger.

"Hello Norbert, I was just looking for you! What have you got there?"

"I've just found this nest," Norbert said.
"It doesn't seem to belong to anyone.
And look at these eggs! Aren't they beautiful?"

"They sure are," Ginger answered. "Let's go fishing."

"I can't leave these eggs," Norbert said.
"Besides they'll need to be warm
when they hatch. Why don't you sit
on the nest Ginger? And I'll go fishing,"
said Norbert.

Ginger was surprised but he did not
want to argue with the old wild duck.
"Why not?" he answered.

Over the next few weeks, Ginger sat on the eggs day and night and Norbert brought him worms and small fish to eat.

Finally, four beautiful baby geese cracked the eggs open and came out of their shells.

Ginger was happy to come off the nest and stretch his legs at long last.

"I'll go to the farm!" Ginger said.
"I feel like eating a bowl of
corn for a change!"

"You certainly deserve it," Norbert said.
"Have some fun. I'll take care of the baby geese."

Ginger ran to the farm.
He was keen to tell his friends
about his adventure.

Soon everyone in the farmyard
knew he that had hatched
four beautiful eggs.

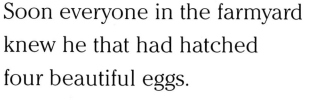

When Mr and Mrs Pinchbeak heard the news they were delighted.
"Show us where they are, Ginger!" they begged.
"They must be our babies. How lucky we are
that Rick the Fox didn't eat them up!"

Led by Ginger, the Pinchbeaks and
their friends slipped through
the fence and went to the pond.

Since Ginger had gone, Norbert
was taking care of the baby geese.
First he cleaned the broken shells
out of the nest, then preened their
down with the tip of his beak.
He brought them worms and he
played with them. How lovely
they were and how soft too!

"Come on, kids, let's go out
and play," he told them.
"Let's pretend we are being
chased and we have to hide."

"Oh yes!" the baby geese shouted.
They hopped out of the nest
and started following the old
wild duck, stumbling along on
their little legs.

They played for a long time. When night fell the little ones were tired so Norbert hid them under a big bush and told them not to make a sound.

The moon rose in the sky,
clear and shining. "I'm worried,"
Norbert said to himself.
"This is a perfect night
for foxes to go hunting."

Norbert gathered the baby geese closer to him and pricked up his ears. Soon he heard a noise... lots of noise!

It sounded like an army on the march!

Oh no! Rick the Fox had found them!
His sense of smell had led him from
the pond to the bushes.

Rick loomed above Norbert and the baby geese, his big green eyes shining like a pair of twin moons.

"Nice try, Norbert!" said Rick. "But foxes are smarter than ducks, that's why we eat them and not the other way round. Didn't you know that?"

Norbert tried to flap his wings to scare Rick away but he could see that he was no match for his old enemy…

…then all of a sudden
Hamlet the Pig
leaped out of the
bushes followed by
Mr and Mrs Pinchbeak,
Ginger and Cluck-Cluck
the Hen.

They all jumped on Rick and chased him into the woods beyond the pond and far away from the farm, until they were sure he would never come back again.

"I don't know how to thank you, Norbert,"
Mrs Pinchbeak said, wiping away a tear.
"Without you Rick would have eaten our babies."
"I was very happy to help," Norbert said.
"You're very welcome," added Ginger.

Back on the farm, the wild duck said farewell to the baby geese.

"We had fun playing, didn't we, Norbert?

We didn't scream and we didn't make a lot of noise either."

"You were great!" said Norbert.

"Now I've got to go. I'm a wild duck
you know. I can't stay on the farm."
Flapping his wings Norbert took off.

"Will he teach us how to fly when
he comes back?" the baby geese
asked their mother.

"I'm sure he will," said Mrs Pinchbeak.
"That will be your next big adventure!"